The Loudest Roar

Thomas Taylor

OXFORD
UNIVERSITY PRESS

The jungle was a peaceful place.
Everyone was quiet. Everyone was calm.

Well, nearly everyone.

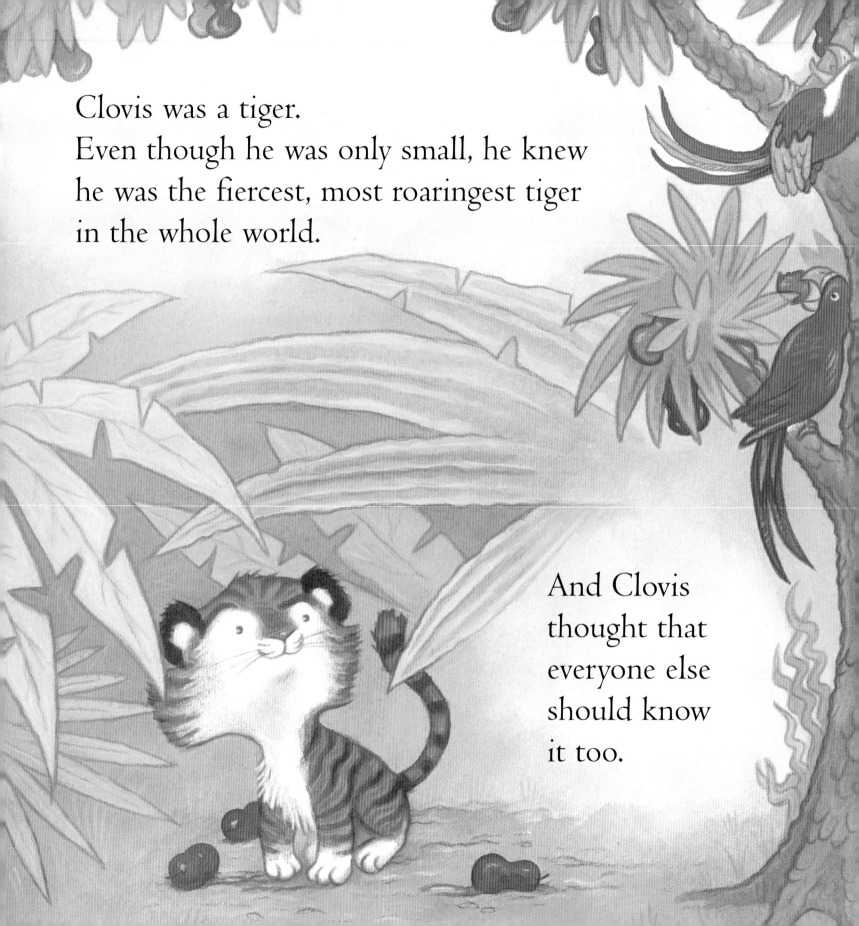

Clovis was a tiger.
Even though he was only small, he knew
he was the fiercest, most roaringest tiger
in the whole world.

And Clovis
thought that
everyone else
should know
it too.

One day, he saw some parrots
chatting politely as they
picked their juicy fruit.

ROAR!

Suddenly - there was Clovis!

He found some muddy wildebeest
wallowing happily in their slimy swamp.

They didn't see the roaringest tiger
in the whole world.

ROOr

Then, suddenly - there was Clovis!

The mighty elephants
were sunning themselves
peacefully at
the edge of
the jungle.

ARRR!

Suddenly - there was Clovis!

'Oh, yes,' said Clovis proudly. 'I've got the loudest roar in all the jungle.'

The animals began to complain. 'Why should he spoil our peace?' squawked an angry parrot.

But what could they do?
Then a monkey, who was
very clever, had an idea.

Clovis didn't notice

the others

creeping up

on him.

Then,
suddenly...

Clovis was
very surprised.

It was the
loudest
roar he had
ever heard.

The little monkey
looked up at the fiercest,
most roaringest tiger in the world.
'If you promise not to roar at us,' he said,
'then we promise not to roar at you.'
Clovis said he would try.

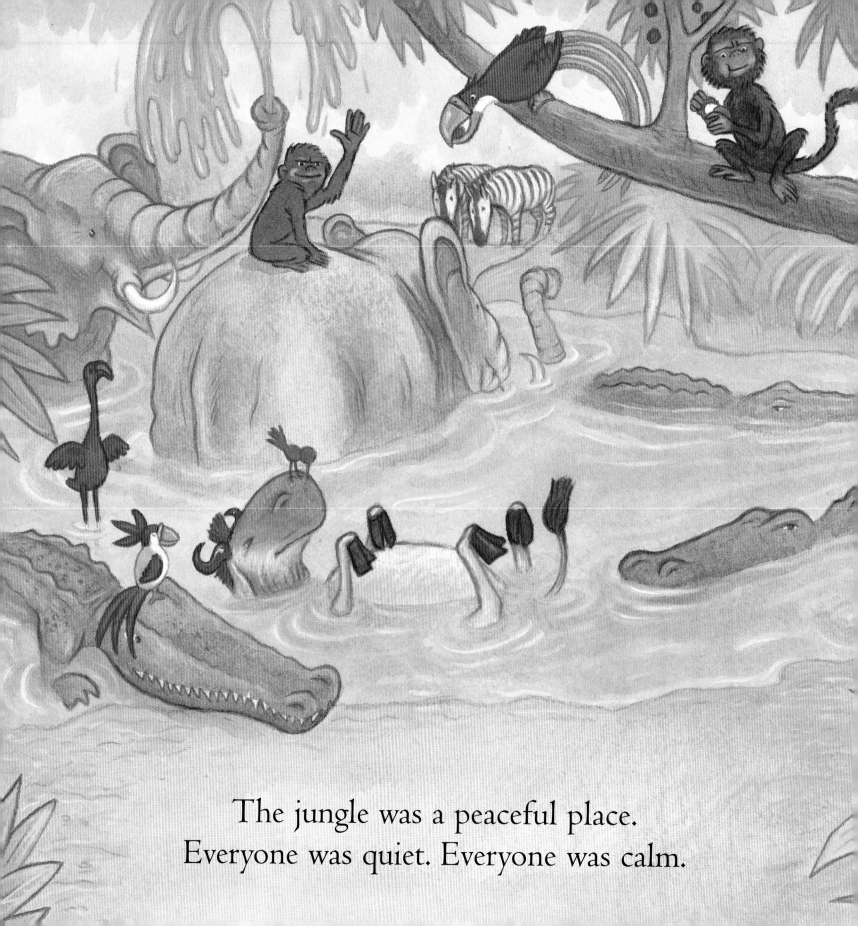

The jungle was a peaceful place.
Everyone was quiet. Everyone was calm.

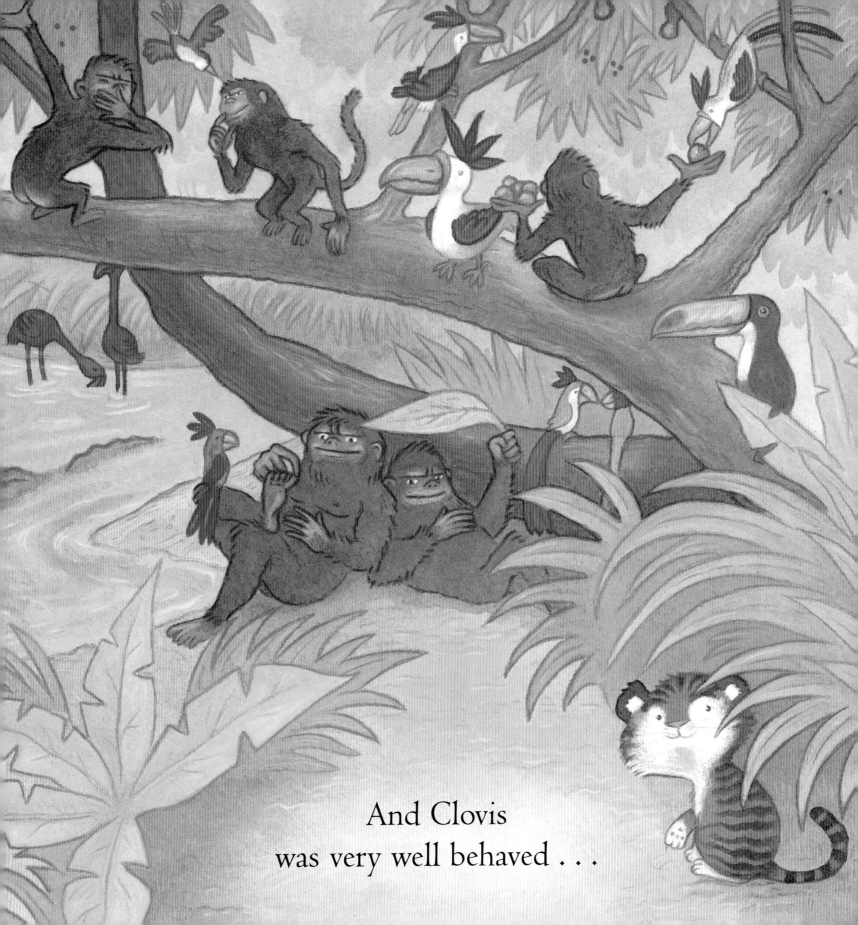

And Clovis
was very well behaved . . .

. . . most of the time.

UNIVERSITY PRESS

Great Clarendon Street, Oxford OX2 6DP

Oxford University Press is a department of the University of Oxford.
It furthers the University's objective of excellence in research, scholarship,
and education by publishing worldwide in

Oxford New York

Auckland Bangkok Buenos Aires Cape Town Chennai
Dar es Salaam Delhi Hong Kong Istanbul Karachi Kolkata
Kuala Lumpur Madrid Melbourne Mexico City Mumbai Nairobi
São Paulo Shanghai Singapore Taipei Tokyo Toronto
with an associated company in Berlin

Oxford is a registered trade mark of Oxford University Press
in the UK and in certain other countries

British Library Cataloguing in Publication Data available

ISBN 0 19 279082 X (hardback)
ISBN 0 19 272518 1 (paperback)

1 3 5 7 9 10 8 6 4 2

Printed in Singapore by Imago